W9-BSD-358

THE AFRICAN RHINOS

BY
WILLIAM R. SANFORD
CARL R. GREEN

EDITED BY
DR. HOWARD SCHROEDER
**Professor in Reading and Language Arts
Dept. of Elementary Education
Mankato State University**

PRODUCED AND DESIGNED BY
BAKER STREET PRODUCTIONS
Mankato, MN

CRESTWOOD HOUSE
Mankato, Minnesota

PROPERTY OF
ST. FELIX COMMUNITY LIBRARY
WABASHA, MINN.

CIP

LIBRARY OF CONGRESS CATALOGING IN PUBLICATION DATA

Sanford, William R. (William Reynolds).
The African rhinos.

(Wildlife, habits & habitat)
"Baker Street Productions."
Includes Index.
SUMMARY:

ISBN 0-89686-327-1

International Standard Book Number:	Library of Congress Catalog Card Number:
Library Binding 0-89686-327-1	

ILLUSTRATION CREDITS:

Cover Photo: Fawcett/Tom Stack & Associates
Lynn M. Stone: 4, 7, 10, 13, 16, 29, 36
Stephen J. Krasemann/DRK Photo: 9, 19, 20, 39
Jim Brandenburg/DRK Photo: 14, 24-25, 30, 35, 40, 45
Bob Williams: 26
Leonard Lee Rue III: 32
Phil & Loretta Hermann: 43

Copyright© 1987 by Crestwood House, Inc. All rights reserved. No part of this book may be reproduced in any form without written permission from the publisher, except for brief passages included in a review. Printed in the United States of America.

CRESTWOOD HOUSE

Hwy. 66 South, Box 3427
Mankato, MN 56002-3427

TABLE OF CONTENTS

This odd-looking animal is an African black rhinoceros.

INTRODUCTION:

The station wagon rolled to a stop beside a metal fence. In the distance, lions roared. Five zebras trotted by, but the girls in the car didn't see them. They were staring at a giraffe.

"This is the best birthday party I've ever had!" Caroline shouted. "Thanks for bringing us to Wild Animal Park, Bob." She hugged her brother. "This is like being on an African safari."

"What do you think of this big fellow?" Bob asked. He pointed at a large, blackish-grey animal that was nibbling on a bush near the fence. "I'm writing a paper about these animals for my college zoology class."

"Except for his short legs, he's almost as big as an elephant," Caroline said. "What is that odd-looking animal?"

"That's a rhinopotamus," Tammy said from the back seat.

"You're close," Bob laughed. "It's an African black rhinoceros. If you look closely, you'll see two more taking a mud bath over there by the trees. Call 'em rhinos for short."

The rhino looked at the girls from black eyes that seemed too small for his big head. The two horns on his snout made him look rather dangerous.

"By the way, you're also looking at a unicorn," Bob added.

"That's going too far!" Sara said. "I've seen pictures of unicorns. They were white horses with long, straight horns growing out of their foreheads—if they existed at all."

Bob reached into a cooler and handed out cold drinks. "Let's take a break for a minute while I study my friend here. If you like, I'll tell you why the rhino is also a unicorn."

The rhinoceros went back to munching on the bush while the girls sipped their drinks. Bob made sketches on a drawing pad.

"It all started with the ancient Greeks," Bob said. "They believed that the unicorn had magic powers. One touch of a unicorn's horn, for example, was supposed to turn bad water into safe drinking water. Later on, the Greeks decided that drinking from a unicorn horn would keep them safe from poison. It was only a short jump to the belief that the horn will cure disease."

"But unicorns are fairy tale animals!" Caroline said.

"That didn't stop people from buying what they thought were unicorn horns," Bob told her. "After all, no one knew what a unicorn actually looked like. For example, Marco Polo thought the rhino he saw in Sumatra in the 1300's was a live unicorn. After all, it did have a horn growing on its head."

Caroline looked at the rhino's two sharp horns. "So people killed rhinos for their horns, just as they killed elephants for their tusks," she said sadly.

"The killing is still going on," Bob said. "Many

People kill many rhinos for the horns.

people in Asia and Africa believe that rhino horns have magic powers. It's sad, because rhino-horn medicines don't seem to cure anything.''

''Let's stop at the gift shop on the way out,'' Caroline told her brother as he started the engine. ''I'm going to buy a book about rhinos. I can't have you knowing more than I do about such an interesting animal.''

CHAPTER ONE:

Imagine that you're on a photo safari in East Africa. Suddenly, an animal the size of a small truck crashes out of a clump of brush. Small, piggy eyes seem fixed on your chest! As you dive to the side, the ground trembles under the weight of the galloping beast. Your guide grabs his rifle and whacks the animal on the side of the head. It bellows and trots away.

You've just met an African rhinoceros. Rhinos will charge almost anything—a strange noise, a lion, or even a butterfly. That's one of the reasons hunters say that the rhino is one of the most dangerous of all game animals. Only poachers (illegal hunters) shoot these huge animals today. They're an endangered species.

Rhinos have a long history

The rhinoceros belongs to a family of mammals that has been on earth for thousands of years. One of its ancestors was the *Baluchitherium,* the largest mammal that ever lived. This giant was eighteen feet tall (5.5 m) and twenty-eight feet (8.5 m) long.

Early rhinos lived everywhere except in Australia, South America, and the polar regions. The rhino vanished from North America thousands of years ago, however. The species lasted longer in Europe, where it was hunted by ancient tribes. Rhinos disappeared from Europe ten thousand years ago, at the time of the last ice age. Today, they're found only in Asia and Africa.

A small family of large animals

The rhinoceros belongs to the *Perissodactyla.* This family includes the horse, wild ass, zebra, and tapir. All of these animals have long heads adapted to eating plants. The name rhinoceros comes from the Greek words *rhino* (nose) and *keras* (horn).

The name rhinoceros comes from the Greek words rhino (nose) and keras (horn).

Of the many species of rhino that once lived, only five remain. Naturalists divide them into one-horned and two-horned varieties. The one-horned rhinos are the Indian rhino and the Javan rhino. One two-horned rhino also lives in Asia—the Sumatran rhino.

The best-known family members are the two-horned African rhinos. They are the black rhino *(Diceros bicornis)* and the white rhino *(Ceratotherium simum)*. These names are misleading, for both animals are a blackish-grey in color. The white rhino's name comes from the Dutch word, *wijde* (wide). The name likely refers to the white rhino's wide, squared-off upper lip.

The white rhino has a wide, squared-off upper lip that allows the white rhino to graze on grass close to the ground.

No one knows exactly how the black rhino earned its name. Perhaps, naturalists say, it's simply the opposite of white.

An endangered species

At one time, rhinos existed in great numbers. Today, all five rhinos are on the endangered species list. The Sumatran and Javan rhinos are in the greatest danger. Naturalists believe that there are only three hundred Sumatran rhinos alive, and as few as fifty Javan rhinos. Similarly, the Indian rhino has almost vanished from its old habitats in India and Nepal. Its numbers are down to about 1,500.

The African varieties face the same danger. Counting those in captivity, only about three thousand white rhinos are alive today. The black rhinos have been reduced to about nine thousand. Only a century or so ago, rhinos were numerous all through eastern and southern Africa. Since then, people have killed about ninety-five percent of the African rhinos, mostly for their horns.

Second largest land mammal

All rhinos have large heads and short necks. They carry their barrel-shaped bodies on short, stumpy legs.

The males (called bulls) are larger than the females (the cows). Among land mammals, only elephants are larger than the white rhino.

Rhinos vary greatly in size. The smallest rhino is the Sumatran, which weighs an average of 1,850 pounds (840 kg). The Javan rhino weighs in at 4,000 pounds (1,814 kg), and the Indian rhino averages 4,200 pounds (1,905 kg). The black rhino weighs over 2,500 pounds (1,134 kg). The blacks are dwarfed by the white rhino's seven thousand pounds (3,175 kg), however. If that's not big enough, the largest white rhinos weigh up to five tons or ten thousand pounds (4,536 kg)!

White and black rhinos have other differences. Black rhinos stand about five feet (1.5 m) tall and can reach twelve feet (3.7 m) in length. Their larger white cousins often grow to over seven feet (2.13 m) tall. White rhinos have a large hump on their backs, but black rhinos do not.

Although rhinos look clumsy, they are fast and agile on their stumpy legs and three-toed feet. Each foot is about twelve inches (30 cm) in diameter. Most of the weight is carried by the large center toe. A close look at the rhino's foot shows that each toe has a hoof like the hooves of a horse. A fourth toe on each front foot is called the rudimentary toe. It is "left over" from earlier times in the rhino's development, and is no longer used.

A tough, flexible grey skin

African rhinos range in color from a light ash grey to almost black. The skin on the underside is almost always lighter in color. Black rhinos are darker in color than the white rhinos, but not by much. Both species are completely hairless, except for a fringe of hair on the tail and ears.

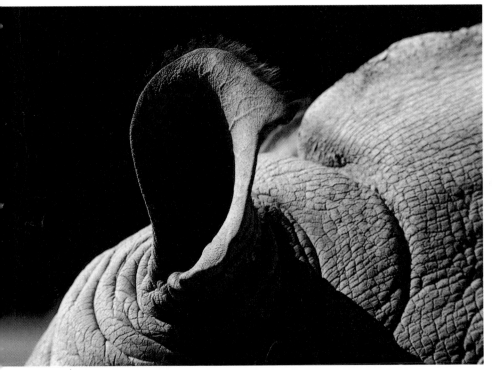

Both species of rhino, the black and white, are completely hairless except for the tail and ears.

PROPERTY OF
ST. FELIX GRADE SCHOOL LIBRARY
WABASHA, MINN.

At first glance, a rhino looks as if its skin is a size too big. The loose-fitting skin lies in folds on the neck and above the legs. Black rhinos have deep grooves at the neck and across their ribs. The white rhino's skin is smoother. The tough, flexible skin protects the animals from thorns and insects.

A horn made from long fibers

Most animals grow their horns or antlers on top of their heads. Rhinos are different. They grow their horns on top of their long snouts. The horns differ in other

The horns of the rhino are different from other animals. The rhino's horns grow on top of its long snout.

ways, too. A Cape buffalo's horns, for example, are made of solid keratin (the material found in fingernails) with a pithy core. A rhino's two horns, by contrast, are made up of keratin fibers, or modified hairs. The spaghetti-like fibers are cemented together in layers. The horns splinter and break easily, but new horns grow quickly.

The front horn is almost always the longest. The black rhino's front horn averages twenty inches (51 cm) in length. The white rhino's longer horns are usually about twenty-four inches (61 cm). The record horns are much longer: forty-four inches (112 cm) for black rhinos and sixty-five inches (165 cm) for white rhinos. A very few black rhinos have three horns.

A rhino uses its horns in several ways. First, the horns are deadly weapons. One quick toss of the rhino's powerful neck can drive its horn completely through a hyena or a lion. A bull also uses his horns when he's fighting with other bulls for a mate. Finally, rhinos plow up the earth with their horns after drinking. Naturalists say they're searching for salt and other minerals.

Weak eyes, keen ears and nose

Unlike most grazing animals, the rhinoceros has poor eyesight. Beyond thirty feet (9 m), the rhino's world

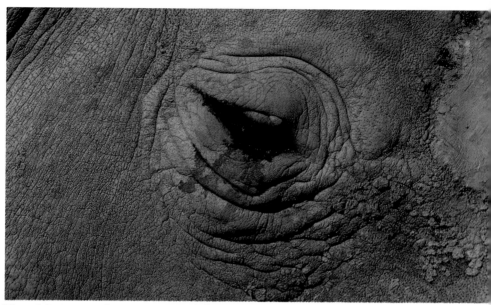
The rhinoceros has poor eyesight.

is a big blur. Even at half that distance, a black rhino can't tell the difference between a hunter and a tree. To make matters worse, the rhino's eyes are set on each side of its head. This keeps it from focusing straight ahead. Its horns also get in the way. If a rhino wants to look at an object that lies directly ahead, it swings its head from side to side.

A rhino makes up for poor eyesight with keen hearing. As soon as it hears a strange noise, it swivels its cone-shaped ears in that direction. Sometimes a rhino will walk a short distance and stop to listen again. That seems to give it a "fix" on the exact source of the sound. A second later, the rhino may run away—or charge directly at the threatening noise. Even when it is resting, a rhino's ears rotate like tiny radar sets.

Most of all, a rhinoceros relies on its nose. Naturalists say that a rhino can pick up the scent of a predator from half a mile (800 m) away. If a cow is separated from her calf, she moves about, sniffing the air all the time. As soon as she picks up the scent, she can find the lost calf. Smell also plays an important role in a rhino's social life. Black rhinos mark off their territory with piles of dung. The scent tells other rhinos to stay away.

Rhinos fill their habitat with sound

Rhinos are one of Africa's most "talkative" animals. They bellow, squeal, growl, grunt, and scream. Their voices range from a deep bass to a high soprano. If the wind brings the scent of danger, their warning snorts sound like explosive sneezes.

The rhino's noises have a purpose. Cows call their wandering calves with a soft, mewing sound. Old bulls scream and snort when they challenge a rival to a fight. The cows even have their own "love song" to attract the bulls during the mating season. With all this "chatter," the rhino's habitat is seldom silent.

CHAPTER TWO:

The rhinoceros once ranged widely over eastern and southern Africa. Today, the last African rhinos are found in a much smaller area. Many exist only in game parks, where the African governments try to protect them from poachers.

The black rhino ranges across east Africa, from the Gulf of Aden south to the Union of South Africa. A few black rhinos also hold on in central Africa (near Lake Chad) and west Africa (in Angola). The best habitat for black rhinos is in thorny brush country, near streams and water holes. In Kenya, black rhinos are found in mountain forests up to the seven-thousand-foot (2,134 m) level.

The white rhino is now confined to only two areas. The last remaining animals live either in South Africa or in the border region between Sudan, Uganda, and Zaire. The white rhinos prefer to graze on open grasslands (called savannahs). When they want to rest or find shade, they retreat into dense brush.

A diet of plants

An animal that weighs four thousand pounds (1,814 kg) or more must consume huge quantities of food. For the rhino, that means almost constant eating during the early evening, throughout the night and early morning. Because the rhino is a herbivore, it eats only grass, leaves, and twigs. Medium-sized rhinos kept in zoos eat at least fifty pounds (22.7 kg) of hay each day!

Black and white rhinos have different eating habits. The black rhino is a browsing animal. It bites off branches, vines, bark, and leaves from nearly two hundred different plants. When they're hungry, black rhinos will even eat thorn bushes. The rhino uses its flexible upper lip to stuff food into its mouth. Then it shears the branches off like an electric hedge clipper. Powerful molars grind each mouthful into small bits.

By contrast, the white rhino is a grazing animal. It moves through a field of tall grass like a lawnmower. Its squared-off mouth cuts off big mouthfuls of grass near the roots. Both species smack their lips and grunt loudly while they're feeding.

The black rhino uses it's upper lip to stuff grass into its mouth while the white rhino (right) has a squared-off mouth and eats like a lawnmower.

Never too far
from water

All rhinos like to stay within a few miles of their water holes. They travel there early each day to drink their fill. If the water holes dry up, the rhino can survive for a long time on moisture-rich plants.

While they're at the water hole, rhinos also enjoy a good wallow. Any muddy patch will do. The rhino lies down in the mud and rolls from side to side. When it leaves the wallow, the rhino is covered with mud. Depending on the soil, a mud-covered rhino may look brick red, greyish white, or several colors at once.

Rhinos love a good mud bath.

Wallowing is more than good fun. The caked-on mud protects the rhino's skin from ticks and biting insects. In addition, the mud keeps the animal's skin from drying out. Rhinos also wallow in dust and sand. As they wiggle and roll, dust sprays up in great clouds. After a morning wallow, the rhinos look for a cool spot in which to take a nap.

Not a social animal

Unlike the herd animals, rhinos never gather in large groups. Most black rhinos, in fact, live by themselves. Only at the water holes and during the mating season do these bad-tempered animals put up with one another's company. White rhinos are more even-tempered. Small family groups of six or seven white rhinos sometimes share a fertile savannah.

A black rhino that enters another's territory must be ready for a fight. Both bulls and cows will try to drive the stranger away. The face-off is an awesome sight. The animals lower their heads, scream, and paw the earth. If the stranger doesn't back down, the defender will charge. That's usually enough to send the new-comer running in the other direction. If the newcomer wins, the defeated rhino leaves the area.

The bulls also battle for mates and to test each other's bravery. The fight starts with loud snorts and much pawing of the ground. If neither backs down, they charge with heads lowered and horns ready. Each bull tries to turn sharply so as to catch the other bull from the side. The bull that gains an advantage will draw blood with his sharp horns. Sometimes the bulls lock horns and try to push each other backward. The bulls don't fight to the death, however. The loser breaks off the fight and runs away.

Faster than they look

Despite their size and weight, rhinos are quick on their feet. Their fast gaits are the trot and the gallop. White rhinos also canter, using a gait between the trot and the gallop. A trotting rhino moves its feet two at a time: left front and right rear, then right front and left rear. In a canter or a gallop, the rhino springs forward off its rear feet. All four feet leave the ground at the same time.

Rhinos usually take it easy. If they're heading for a water hole, they may walk along at a slow three miles per hour (5 kph). But a smell of danger can change that slow pace to a gallop in an instant. The rhino's head goes down and its tail goes up. A typical gallop reaches twenty-five miles per hour (40 kph). A very fast black rhino has been clocked at forty-five miles per hour (72 kph) for a short distance.

Partners and enemies

Egrets, oxpeckers, and mynas perch on the rhino's back. The birds pay for their ride by cleaning up the rhino's ticks and insects. The birds also serve as an early warning system. When another animal approaches, the birds sound the alarm as they fly away. Some of the birds, however, pick at the rhino's wounds and sores. This keeps the sores from healing, causing infections and possible death.

The rhino ignores most animals. Only a full-grown elephant will pose a threat to this aggressive giant. Lions, hyenas, leopards, and other predators will attack an unprotected rhino calf. Wallowing can also be dangerous. A big rhino sometimes sinks so deeply into the mud that it can't climb out again.

Like other wild animals, rhinos suffer from parasites and liver ailments. Ticks, worms, and other small invaders slow them down but seldom kill them. Despite all these dangers, wild rhinos have been known to live for thirty to forty years.

Naturalists think twice before they go into the field to study the black rhinoceros. The task is always risky, for the nearsighted rhino will charge anything that disturbs it. Despite the problems, naturalists have learned a great deal about the animal's life cycle.

These white rhino were photographed in their habitat in Namibia, Africa.

CHAPTER THREE:

The sun is just rising over Tanzania's Selous Game Reserve. A jeep driven by two naturalists bumps slowly across the grassy plain. "Kifaro and Sweetie should be over in that clump of brush," one of the scientists whispers. "I named the rhinos in this area when I started this study a year ago. Kifaro wants to mate, but Sweetie has been putting him off."

Naturalists and game wardens continually monitor endangered species to ensure their survival.

Just then, a black rhino steps out of the brush. Kifaro trots forward, his head lowered. He heard the jeep long before he could see it. The driver sees him and swings the jeep in a big circle. Kifaro watches the retreat. Then he snorts and turns back to his mate.

Mating and calving

Sweetie is making a whistling sound that attracts the big bull. Kifaro takes some little dancing steps. Then he pushes his large head against the cow's back. At first, she backs away and paws at the dirt. Kifaro doesn't give up. Sweetie retreats again, and still Kifaro follows her. Finally, she stands still and allows him to mate with her.

The naturalists have gone on to watch a cow named Dicey. This time they are able to creep up close without alarming her. At four years of age, Dicey is carrying her first calf. She mated with Kifaro eighteen months ago, and it's time for her calf to be born. Among land mammals, only elephants carry their calves for a longer period.

Dicey gives birth to a female calf in the cool of the evening. Watching from his hiding place, the naturalist names her Raya. At birth, Raya weighs eighty-five pounds (38.6 kg). The shiny skin of her snout doesn't show any trace of a horn. Ten minutes later, Raya tries to stand up. She is still weak, and she falls several times. Finally, she makes it to her feet. Standing on shaky legs, she measures eighteen inches (46 cm) at the shoulder.

Within thirty minutes, Raya walks shakily to the cow's side. She rubs her nose on Dicey's neck. Then she searches for one of her mother's two teats. When she finds it, she takes her first mouthful of milk.

A careful mother

Dicey keeps Raya hidden in the brush for the first few weeks. When Raya is a month old, the cow allows her to move about with her as she browses. The calf never wanders more than a few feet from her mother's side. Kifaro comes nosing around one day, but Dicey quickly drives him away. She does the same thing when a lioness comes prowling by. Dicey would charge an entire pride of lions if the big cats were threatening her calf.

Raya starts feeding on leaves and twigs when she's a week old. She'll keep on feeding from the teat for at least a year, however. During the year, Raya will learn the skills she'll need as an adult. She'll feed from the best plants, bathe, wallow, and avoid danger.

When Dicey goes to the water hole, Raya follows close behind her. If Dicey senses danger, she pushes Raya ahead of her. Raya often strays from the path, but the cow prods her with gentle nudges of her front horn. Raya's own horns are growing, too. At five months, her front horn is almost two inches (5 cm) long.

The rhino calf never leaves its mother's side in the first few weeks after birth.

Life at the water hole

By her first birthday, Raya is half as big as Dicey. She won't reach full size until she's seven. Because Dicey prefers to live alone, Raya doesn't meet many other rhinos. Once, one of Sweetie's older calves tried to join them. Dicey snorted and quickly drove the young cow away. Kifaro sometimes joins the pair as they move toward a new feeding ground, but that doesn't happen often.

Raya's only contact with other rhinos comes at the water hole. The other adults ignore her, but Raya

The rhino's habitat, filled with the "chatter" of rhinos, is seldom silent.

doesn't seem to mind. Wallowing is a great joy. After she drinks, Raya plunges into the soft mud and rolls happily on her back and sides. If Dicey lets her, she'll stay there for hours.

Dicey leaves Raya alone at the wallow one day. Suddenly, the oxpeckers screech and fly into the trees. Raya smells danger. A pack of hyenas are lined up on the bank. As soon as the calf scrambles to her feet, the hyenas slink away. She's already too big for them.

Staking out a territory

Dicey and Raya stake out their territory. The two rhinos "own" a range of about ten square miles (26 sq. km). As they walk, they mark the boundaries with piles of dung. Afterward, they trample in the dung. That way, they leave a scent trail wherever they walk. Within their territory, Dicey has worn trails through the thorny brush. She finds her way by the scent of the urine she sprays on the brush.

One day, Dicey and Raya are taking a dust bath. When they look up, they see four elephants standing around them. The elephants want the dust wallow for themselves. Like bullies on the playground, they blow trunksful of dust over the rhinos. Then one big bull wraps his trunk around Raya. Luckily, she's too heavy to lift. Dicey squeals and leads her calf away. Rhinos don't have much chance against an elephant's tusks.

An end to childhood

As Raya nears four years of age, her bond with Dicey is very strong. Naturalists have seen young rhinos stay with the bodies of their dead mothers until they die of hunger. Dicey mated again eighteen months ago, however. She is about to give birth and she fears that Raya will harm the newborn.

Dicey butts Raya in the side. The blows hurt the calf. Raya squeals and runs away. Confused by the strange behavior, she soon comes back. Dicey butts her again. Raya doesn't know what to do. Finally, she trots away, never to return.

Raya looks for another companion. She tries to stay with Sweetie, but the older cow jabs her with her sharp horns. Hurt and frightened, Raya wanders on. At last, she finds a young bull who lets her stay with him. When spring comes again, the two will mate. If poachers don't kill her, Raya will soon be ready to start the rhino's life cycle all over again.

The bond between a rhino cow and her calf is very strong.

CHAPTER FOUR:

Most Texas ranchers raise cattle and horses. That's too tame for Tom Mantzel. Tom raises wildebeests, giraffes, ostriches—and black rhinos.

What are two rhinos named Makai and Macora doing on Tom's 1,500-acre Waterfall Ranch? They're part of a plan to save the species. Unless something is done, poachers and loss of habitat may soon kill off Africa's last rhinos.

An expensive project

Early in 1984, two conservation groups sent Tom to South Africa. One of the groups is called Game Conservation International (GAMECOIN). Its members hope that the two rhinos Tom captured in Natal will mate and start a Texas herd. When the herd reaches two hundred, GAMECOIN plans to take some black rhinos back to Africa. By that time, the wild black rhinos may be extinct in their home habitat.

Harry Tennison, GAMECOIN's director, isn't sure that the plan will work. ''I doubt that the poaching problem [in Africa] will ever be solved,'' he says. That hasn't kept GAMECOIN from spending $250,000 (US) to bring Makai and Macora to the United States.

Learning to raise rhinos

Getting ready for the rhinos took some careful planning. Tom's first job was to decide how to keep the rhinos from running away. GAMECOIN gave $180,000 (US) to build barns and strong fences. Rhinos can walk right through a wooden fence, and they'd hurt themselves on barbed wire. Tom designed a fence made of steel pipes set in concrete.

Makai and Macora quickly adjusted to their new home. Makai was a "tiny" 1,500 pounds (680 kg) when she arrived, but she's now a full-grown seven-year-old. Unlike most wild rhinos, she likes humans. Makai nuzzles up to Tom, who rewards her with a snack of live oak branches. Then he scratches her behind the ears. Macora lives nearby, but Tom is keeping the two rhinos apart until it's time for them to mate.

Can rhinos survive in Texas?

Tom doesn't worry about the critics who say that rhinos don't belong in Texas. He reminds his listeners that a number of African animals already are doing well in his home state. Tom also points out that his ranch lies about as far north of the equator as the rhino's homeland lies south of it. Moreover, the ranch's plant life and climate are similar to Natal. The rhinos are even

Birds which help the rhino rid itself of fleas and ticks are the oxpeckers.

feeding on their favorite huisache trees (a type of acacia). The only thing missing, Tom laughs, are tsetse flies and oxpeckers.

The rhinos started out in one-acre paddocks. Veterinarians (animal doctors) watched them carefully. When they settled down, Tom moved them into ten-acre pastures. Later on, he plans to turn them loose on a 100-acre range. He's not in any hurry. The GAME-COIN experts say it will take twenty years to reach the target of two hundred rhinos. Along the way, some of the calves will be sold to zoos and wild animal parks.

Not for hunting

Some Texas ranches let hunters pay to shoot their animals. Tom will never allow rhino hunting on Waterfall Ranch. "I'm not against hunting," he says, "but [shooting a rhino] would be about as sporting as shooting Cat." Cat is Tom's pet Labrador retriever!

Instead of hunting, Tom lets people visit the ranch.

The rhino can be observed in many zoos throughout the world.

"I'm letting tourists drive through," he explains. "But there won't be any hippo boat rides or stuffed camels to sit on and get your picture taken." In fact, Tom doesn't allow tourists to leave their cars. He decided to play it safe after he was almost killed by a sharp-horned African antelope.

The trips through Waterfall Ranch serve two purposes. One goal is to let people see wild animals in a natural habitat. In addition, the money Tom raises will go to educate children about the need to protect wildlife.

A rhino in hog heaven

In the meantime, Tom keeps Makai and Macora hidden in a far corner of the ranch. He visits them several times a week to check on their progress. While he's there, he wets down the soft dirt to make a rhino-sized wallow.

Makai helps out by digging in the mud with her horn. Then she circles the muddy spot before plopping herself down in the ooze. Tom thinks she's happy in her Texas home. "That rhino is in hog heaven," he chuckles.

A second group of black rhinos have found a home on a ranch near McAllen, Texas. Adding more rhinos to the project will speed up the day when they can be returned to Africa.

CHAPTER FIVE:

In the early 1800's, over a million black rhinos lived in Africa below the Sahara. Today, fewer than nine thousand still live in the wild. White rhinos are even closer to extinction. It wasn't disease that almost wiped out the rhinoceros. These huge animals ran into a serious case of human greed.

Rhinos died by the thousands

Until recent times, very few people thought of protecting the rhino. The supply seemed endless, and there was a good market for their horns. African natives killed the rhinos and sold the horns to European traders. By 1900, fewer than one hundred white rhinos were left in South Africa.

The sad story was repeated wherever rhinos lived. In 1876, the British colonial government in Kenya offered money for every rhino that was killed. People responded by shooting thousands of the big beasts. With the rhinos gone, the land was opened to farmers and ranchers.

Farmers and ranchers need the grassland that the rhino live on.

British and other European powers set new laws to help save the rhino from extinction.

A change of policy

In 1910, the British government in Kenya realized that the rhinoceros was in danger of extinction. New laws were passed to protect the rhino. The British joined with other European powers in setting up game parks where wild animals would be safe from hunters. For a while it appeared that the rhino might be saved.

After World War II, a new slaughter began. The former African colonies gained their freedom, but the new governments couldn't protect their wildlife. Farmers pushed into the game parks and destroyed rhino habitat. And, always, the poachers came to collect the precious horns.

The high price of rhino horns

As the supply of rhinos decreased, the demand for rhino horns seemed to increase. The shortage made the horns even more valuable. Between 1974 and 1979, the price soared from $35 (US) a kilo (2.2 lb.) to more than $500 (US) a kilo. That was only a start. In 1985, powdered rhino horn sold for $11,000 (US) a kilo in China.

Poachers earn only $200-$400 (US) per horn. Even so, that's enough to feed an African family for a year. Many poor villagers see poaching as their only chance of making a decent living. Despite the best efforts of the game wardens, the killing goes on.

Medicines and dagger handles

The market in rhino horns is based on the belief that a unicorn horn will cure sickness. The Zulus of Africa still use powdered horn to treat coughs, asthma, and nosebleeds. In Asia, doctors add a few grams of rhino horn to medicines (a gram is 1/26th of an ounce). Asians also drink a rhino horn tea that they believe will reduce high fevers. In India, older men take the powdered horn for a different reason. They believe that it will make them feel young again.

All of these people ignore the fact that rhino horn is made of keratin. Doctors know that keratin doesn't have any medical value. People could get the same benefits by adding fingernail clippings to their medicines!

One-half of the rhino horns go to North Yeman, but not for medical reasons. All the men in that Arab land wear daggers. Those made with rhino horn handles are the most highly prized. When a boy is eleven or twelve, he receives his dagger as a sign of manhood. A rhino horn dagger set with silver and precious stones can cost as much as $10,000 (US).

42

Poachers sell rhino horns to people who believe the horn will cure sickness.

Saving the rhino

Naturalists believe that the last wild rhinos must be moved into protected game parks. That sounds easy to do, but it isn't. Most African countries can't afford enough game wardens to protect the game parks they already have. Even when poachers are caught, they often pay bribes and escape with light fines. In addition, the growing African population needs more farmland. Poor people say that good land shouldn't be wasted on wild animals.

The danger to the rhino is real, but the battle isn't over yet. Naturalists have trapped both black and white rhinos and taken them to areas where they can breed safely. At the same time, African governments are cracking down on poachers.

The world is also rallying to save the rhino. The World Wildlife Fund declared 1979 as the Year of the Rhino. Almost all countries have passed laws against importing products taken from rhinos and other endangered species.

The World Wildlife Fund declared 1979, to be the year of the rhino.

Africa

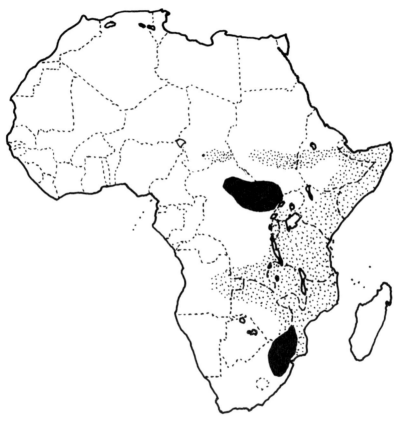

 Most black rhinos live within these areas.

█ Most white rhinos live within these areas.

INDEX/GLOSSARY:

WILDLIFE
HABITS & HABITAT

If you would like to know more about all kinds of wildlife, you should take a look at the other books in this series.

You'll find books on bald eagles and other birds. Books on alligators and other reptiles. There are books about deer and other big-game animals. And there are books about sharks and other creatures that live in the ocean.

In all of the books you will learn that life in the wild is not easy. But you will also learn what people can do to help wildlife survive. So read on!

DEC 2 V

MAR 15
FEB 47

DATE DUE

OCT 12	APR 8		
OCT 13	JAN 12		
NOV 1	MAR 15		
JAN 3	FEB 27		
JAN 24			
FEB 9			
NOV 6			
JAN 17			
SEP 24			
JAN 27			
NOV 17			
DEC 1			
MAY 13			
NOV 1			
OCT 24			
MAY 13			
MAR 24			

Demco, Inc. 38-293